Using the *Literature Circle Guides* in Your Classroom

Each guide contains the following sections:

❋ background information about the author and book

❋ enrichment readings relevant to the book

❋ Literature Response Journal reproducibles

❋ Group Discussion reproducibles

❋ Individual and group projects

❋ Literature Discussion Evaluation Sheet

Background Information and Enrichment Readings

The background information about the author and the book and the enrichment readings are designed to offer information that will enhance students' understanding of the book. You may choose to assign and discuss these sections before, during, or after the reading of the book. Because each enrichment concludes with questions that invite students to connect it to the book, you can use this section to inspire students to think and record their thoughts in the literature response journal.

Literature Response Journal Reproducibles

Although these reproducibles are designed for individual students, they should also be used to stimulate and support discussions in literature circles. Each page begins with a reading strategy and follows with several journal topics. At the bottom of the page, students select a type of response (question, prediction, observation, or connection) for free-choice writing in their response journals.

◆ Reading Strategies

Since the goal of the literature circle is to empower lifelong readers, a different reading strategy is introduced in each section. Not only does the reading strategy allow students to understand this particular book better, but it also instills a habit of mind that will continue to be useful when they read other books. A question from the Literature Response Journal and the Group Discussion pages is always tied to the reading strategy.

If everyone in class is reading the same book, you may present the reading strategy as a mini-lesson to the entire class. For literature circles, however, the group of students can read over and discuss the strategy together at the start of class and then experiment with the strategy as they read silently for the rest of the period. You may want to allow time at the end of class so the group can talk about what they noticed as they read. As an alternative, the literature circle can review the reading strategy for the next section after they have completed their discussion. That night, students can try out the reading strategy as they read on their own so they will be ready for the next day's literature circle discussion.

◆ Literature Response Journal Topics

A literature response journal allows a reader to "converse" with a book. Students write questions, point out things they notice about the story, recall personal experiences, and make connections to other texts in their journals. In other words, they are using writing to explore what they think about the book. See page 7 for tips on how to help students set up their literature response journals.

1. The questions for the literature response journals have no right or wrong answers but are designed to help students look beneath the surface of the plot and develop a richer connection to the story and its characters.

2. Students can write in their literature response journals as soon as they have finished a reading assignment. Again, you may choose to have students do this for homework or make time during class.

3. The literature response journals are an excellent tool for students to use in their literature circles. They can highlight ideas and thoughts in their journals that they want to share with the group.

4. When you evaluate students' journals, consider whether they have completed all the assignments and have responded in depth and thoughtfully. You may want to check each day to make sure students are keeping up with the assignments. You can read and respond to the journals at a halfway point (after five entries) and again at the end. Some teachers suggest that students pick out their five best entries for a grade.

Group Discussion Reproducibles

These reproducibles are designed for use in literature circles. Each page begins with a series of discussion questions for the group to consider. A mini-lesson on an aspect of the writer's craft follows the discussion questions. See page 8 for tips on how to model good discussions for students.

◆ **Literature Discussion Questions:** In a literature discussion, students experience a book from different points of view. Each reader brings her or his own unique observations, questions, and associations to the text. When students share their different reading experiences, they often come to a wider and deeper understanding than they would have reached on their own.

The discussion is not an exercise in finding the right answers nor is it a debate. Its goal is to explore the many possible meanings of a book. Be sure to allow enough time for these conversations to move beyond easy answers—try to schedule 25–35 minutes for each one. In addition, there are important guidelines to ensure that everyone's voice is heard.

1. Let students know that participation in the literature discussion is an important part of their grade. You may choose to watch one discussion and grade it. (You can use the Literature Discussion Evaluation Sheet on page 33.)

2. Encourage students to evaluate their own performance in discussions using the Literature Discussion Evaluation Sheet. They can assess not only their own level of involvement but also how the group itself has functioned.

3. Help students learn how to talk to one another effectively. After a discussion, help them process what worked and what didn't. Videotape discussions if possible, and then evaluate them together. Let one literature circle watch another and provide feedback to it.

4. It can be helpful to have a facilitator for each discussion. The facilitator can keep students from interrupting each other, help the conversation get back on track when it digresses, and encourage shyer members to contribute. At the end of each discussion, the facilitator can summarize everyone's contributions and suggest areas for improvement.

5. Designate other roles for group members. For instance, a recorder can take notes and/or list questions for further discussion. A summarizer can open each literature circle meeting by summarizing the chapter(s) the group has just read. Encourage students to rotate these roles, as well as that of the facilitator.

◆ **The Writer's Craft:** This section encourages students to look at the writer's most important tool—words. It points out new vocabulary, writing techniques, and uses of language. One or two questions invite students to think more deeply about the book and writing in general. These questions can either become part of the literature circle discussion or be written about in students' journals.

Literature Discussion Evaluation Sheet

Both you and your students will benefit from completing these evaluation sheets. You can use them to assess students' performance, and as mentioned above, students can evaluate their own individual performances, as well as their group's performance. The Literature Discussion Evaluation Sheet appears on page 33.

Literature Circle Guide:
Maniac Magee

by Perdita Finn

S C H O L A S T I C
PROFESSIONAL BOOKS

New York • Toronto • London • Auckland • Sydney
• Mexico City • New Delhi • Hong Kong

Guide written by Perdita Finn
Edited by Sarah Glasscock
Cover design by Niloufar Safavieh
Interior design by Grafica, Inc.
Interior illustrations by Mona Mark

Credits: Jacket cover from MANIAC MAGEE by Jerry Spinelli. Cover photograph by Carole Palmer. Cover copyright © 1992 by HarperCollins Publishers. Reprinted by permission of HarperCollins Publishers. Interior: Author photo on page 9 courtesy of Delacourt Press, New York, NY.

ISBN 0-439-16362-5

Printed in the U.S.A.

Contents

To the Teacher

As a teacher, you naturally want to instill in your students the habits of confident, critical, independent, and lifelong readers. You hope that even when students are not in school they will seek out books on their own, think about and question what they are reading, and share those ideas with friends. An excellent way to further this goal is by using literature circles in your classroom.

In a literature circle, students select a book to read as a group. They think and write about it on their own in a literature response journal and then discuss it together. Both journals and discussions enable students to respond to a book and develop their insights into it. They also learn to identify themes and issues, analyze vocabulary, recognize writing techniques, and share ideas with each other—all of which are necessary to meet state and national standards.

This guide provides the support materials for using literature circles with *Maniac Magee* by Jerry Spinelli. The reading strategies, discussion questions, projects, and enrichment readings will also support a whole class reading of this text or can be given to enhance the experience of an individual student reading the book as part of a reading workshop.

Literature Circles

A literature circle consists of several students (usually three to five) who agree to read a book together and share their observations, questions, and interpretations. Groups may be organized by reading level or choice of book. Often these groups read more than one book together since, as students become more comfortable talking with one another, their observations and insights deepen.

When planning to use literature circles in your classroom, it can be helpful to do the following:

* Recommend four or five books from which students can choose. These books might be grouped by theme, genre, or author.

* Allow three or four weeks for students to read each book. Each of Scholastic's *Literature Circle Guides* has ten sections as well as enrichment activities and final projects. Even if students are reading different books in the *Literature Circle Guide* series, they can be scheduled to finish at the same time.

* Create a daily routine so students can focus on journal writing and discussions.

* Decide whether students will be reading books in class or for homework. If students do all their reading for homework, then allot class time for sharing journals and discussions. You can also alternate silent reading and writing days in the classroom with discussion groups.

Read More About Literature Circles

Getting the Most from Literature Groups by Penny Strube (Scholastic Professional Books, 1996)

Literature Circles by Harvey Daniels (Stenhouse Publishers, 1994)

Setting Up Literature Response Journals

Although some students may already keep literature response journals, others may not know how to begin. To discourage students from merely writing elaborate plot summaries and to encourage them to use their journals in a meaningful way, help them focus their responses around the following elements: predictions, observations, questions, and connections.

Have students take time after each assigned section to think about and record their responses in their journals. Sample responses appear below.

◆ **Predictions:** Before students read the book, have them study the cover and the jacket copy. Ask if anyone has read any other books by Jerry Spinelli. To begin their literature response journals, tell students to jot down their impressions about the book. As they read, students will continue to make predictions about what a character might do or how the plot might turn. After finishing the book, students can re-assess their initial predictions. Good readers understand that they must constantly activate prior knowledge before, during, and after they read. They adjust their expectations and predictions; a book that is completely predictable is not likely to capture anyone's interest. A student about to read *Maniac Magee* for the first time might predict the following:

I know the word maniac *can mean "crazy." But it can also be used to describe somebody who's really focused on something, like my dad. He's a maniac about model airplanes. I can't tell yet what the name means in this book. It depends on who gave Jeffrey the nickname "Maniac."*

◆ **Observations:** This activity takes place immediately after reading begins. In a literature response journal, the reader recalls fresh impressions about the characters, setting, and events. Most readers mention details that stand out for them, even if they are not sure what their importance is. For example, a reader might list phrases that describe how a character looks or the feeling a setting evokes. Many readers note certain words, phrases, or passages in a book. Others note the style of an author's writing or the voice in which the story is told. A student just starting to read *Maniac Magee* might write the following:

I noticed the writer starts every sentence with "they say" so it's like all the crazy things that follow might not be true at all. He writes like he lives in the neighborhood and knows everything he's talking about, but I don't know everything. He mentions Little League, so maybe this story has something to do with baseball.

◆ **Questions:** Point out that good readers don't necessarily understand everything they read. To clarify their uncertainty, they ask questions. Encourage students to identify passages that confuse or trouble them and emphasize that they shouldn't take anything for granted. Share the following student example:

What is the writer talking about??? I can't follow any of this! Who is Finsterwald? And what's a clump of string got to do with anything? What's this East Side/West Side stuff? Who is Maniac Magee anyway?

◆ **Connections:** Remind students that one story often leads to another. When one friend tells a story, the other friend is often inspired to tell one, too. The same thing often happens when someone reads a book. A character reminds the reader of a relative, or a situation is similar to something that happened to him or her. Sometimes a book makes a reader recall other books or movies. These connections can be helpful in revealing some of the deeper meanings or patterns of a book. The following is an example of a student connection:

All the "they say" stuff reminds me of this kid called Big Wallace who was supposed to go to my school once. I heard he got in a fight every day in the cafeteria and they say he made that big hole in the concrete in the front of the building. It's always the older kids who say stuff like that.

The Good Discussion

In a good literature discussion, students are always learning from one another. They listen to one another and respond to what their peers have to say. They share their ideas, questions and observations. Everyone feels comfortable about talking, and no one interrupts or puts down what anyone else says. Students leave a good literature discussion with a new understanding of the book—and sometimes with new questions about it. They almost always feel more engaged by what they have read.

◆ **Modeling a Good Discussion:** In this era of combative and confessional TV talk shows, students often don't have any idea of what it means to talk productively and creatively together. You can help them have a better idea of what a good literature discussion is if you let them experience one. Select a thought-provoking short story or poem for students to read, and then choose a small group to model a discussion of the work for the class.

Explain to participating students that the objective of the discussion is to explore the text thoroughly and learn from one another. Emphasize that it takes time to learn how to have a good discussion, and that the first discussion may not achieve everything they hope it will. Duplicate a copy of the Literature Discussion Evaluation Sheet for each student. Go over the helpful and unhelpful contributions shown on the Literature Discussion Evaluation Sheet. Instruct students to fill it out as they watch the model discussion. Then have the group of students hold its discussion while the rest of the class observes. Try not to interrupt or control the discussion and remind the student audience not to participate. It's okay if the discussion falters, as this is a learning experience.

Allow 15–20 minutes for the discussion. When it is finished, ask each student in the group to reflect out loud about what worked and what didn't. Then have the students who observed share their impressions. What kinds of comments were helpful? How could the group have talked to each other more productively? You may want to let another group experiment with a discussion so students can try out what they learned from the first one.

◆ **Assessing Discussions:** The following tips will help students monitor how well their group is functioning:

1. One person should keep track of all behaviors by each group member, both helpful and unhelpful, during the discussion.

2. At the end of the discussion, each individual should think about how he or she did. How many helpful and unhelpful checks did he or she receive?

3. The group should look at the Literature Discussion Evaluation Sheet and assess their performance as a whole. Were most of the behaviors helpful? Were any behaviors unhelpful? How could the group improve?

In good discussions, you will often hear students say the following:
....

"I was wondering if anyone knew . . ."

"I see what you are saying. That reminds me of something that happened earlier in the book."

"What do you think?"

"Did anyone notice on page 57 that . . ."

"I disagree with you because . . ."

"I agree with you because . . ."

"This reminds me so much of when . . ."

"Do you think this could mean . . ."

"I'm not sure I understand what you're saying. Could you explain it a little more to me?"

"That reminds me of what you were saying yesterday about . . ."

"I just don't understand this."

"I love the part that says . . ."

"Here, let me read this paragraph. It's an example of what I'm talking about."

About *Maniac Magee*

Maniac Magee takes off so fast and is so funny from the very first sentence that you can barely catch your breath between laughing and reading. Wildly hilarious yet filled with heart, this story of the miracles young Jeffrey Magee performs in the small town of Two Mills is the all-time favorite story of many kids—and grown-ups, too. Could this be one of the greatest books ever written? You decide!

About the Author: Jerry Spinelli

 Readers often want to know how a writer comes up with ideas. "Everywhere" is author Jerry Spinelli's answer. One day while reading the newspaper, he came across an article about a local girl who was competing on her high school wrestling team. Less than a year later Spinelli had written *There's a Girl in My Hammerlock*. The book *Who Put That Hair in My Toothbrush?* was inspired by the constant squabbling of two of his six kids, Jeffrey and Molly. But most of all, Spinelli seems to draw on memories from his own childhood.

> *I thought I was simply growing up in Norristown, Pennsylvania; looking back now I can see that I was also gathering material that would one day find its way into my books. John Ribble's blazing fastball. Dovey Wilmouth, so beautiful a fleet of boys pedaled past her house ten times a day. Mrs. Seeton's whistle calling her kids in to dinner.*

When Jerry Spinelli was little, he wanted to be a cowboy, and then he dreamed of being the shortstop for the New York Yankees. He played Little League all through junior high and high school, but only hit two home runs in his whole career. One day when Spinelli was sixteen, however, he discovered what he really wanted to do with the rest of his life. The high school football team had won a big game, and while the rest of the town was out celebrating, Jerry Spinelli went home and wrote a poem about it. A few days later the poem was published in the newspaper, and that was it: He knew he wanted to be a writer.

It was a long time before Jerry Spinelli's first book was published. After college, he became an editor for a magazine about engineering and wrote books for adults during his lunch hour. None of them was ever published. Then when Spinelli was forty-one, he wrote *Space Station Seventh Grade* and made his breakthrough as a children's book writer. He was as happy about that first book being published as he was about later winning the Newbery Medal for *Maniac Magee*.

To date, Jerry Spinelli has published sixteen books, but surprisingly he doesn't consider himself a writer.

> *I find that I hesitate to put that label on myself, to define myself by what I do for a living. After all, I also pick berries and touch ponies and skim flat stones over water and marvel at the stars and breathe deeply and grin from ear to ear and save the best part for last. I've always done these things. Which is to say, I never had to become anything. Or anyone. I always, already, was.*

In his latest memoir *Knots in My Yo-Yo String: The Autobiography of a Kid*, Spinelli talks about his childhood memories and the role they play in his writing.

Enrichment: Folk Heroes

If you've ever found yourself telling a true story and beginning to exaggerate just a little, you know how a legend starts. "Why, he must have caught a hundred fish that day," you find yourself saying—not because he really did, but because you want to let your audience know, quickly, that this guy is the greatest fisherman of all time, that he always catches more fish than anybody else. If you say he caught twelve fish, that doesn't sound as impressive as a hundred fish does. By exaggerating, you get your point across. Of course, the next person who tells the story might make it two hundred, and before you know it, the whole thing is snowballing, and that friend of yours is cleaning out the Great Lakes of all their fish.

American history is filled with legends and folk heroes; for example, the story of Paul Bunyan, the giant lumberjack who weighed eighty-six pounds when he was born and later used a pine tree to comb his beard. He dug the Mississippi River and the Great Lakes and created the Grand Canyon when he let his enormous ax drag behind him one day. Stories about Paul Bunyan were passed around among lumbermen in the nineteenth century, and perhaps a real lumberjack inspired the first story about Paul Bunyan. What *is* true is that when America was expanding west, the lumberjacks were clearing roads and cities to help create the country we live in today.

Some folk heroes really did exist—Davy Crockett, Buffalo Bill, and John Henry, most probably—but the stories that grew up around them got wilder and wilder. Take Johnny Appleseed, for example. John Chapman was born in 1774 in Leominster, Massachusetts, and later became a nurseryman who collected apple seeds from cider presses and began selling and giving them away to westward pioneers.

John Chapman was supposed to be one of the most cheerful, generous, and gentle people who ever lived. They say he loved animals so much that one night when he was cooking mush, he

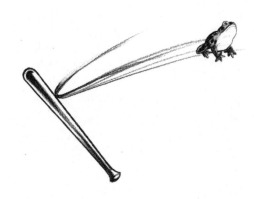

noticed the mosquitoes were buzzing and burning themselves in the flames from his campfire. Chapman poured water on the fire and put it out. "I'll do without a fire, if it means giving hurt to a living critter," he said.

Once he came across a wolf caught in a trap and turned it loose. Later when Chapman was having some trouble with the Shawnee, who thought he was unlike anybody they'd ever seen before, the wolf appeared and started snarling at them. Johnny Chapman started petting the wolf and the Shawnee, convinced he was a shaman (medicine man), gave him the run of their camp. Eventually, Chapman was welcomed by everyone. He cared for the sick, always loved to play with the children, and carried news from settlement to settlement.

When he was old and about to die, it is said he had a dream of all his apple trees in blossom along a riverbank with the fox and the rabbits, the panther and the deer all playing together. There were Indians and white people and people of all colors, laughing and having a good time together. "It's a dream," said Johnny, "But it needn't be."

As Jerry Spinelli says at the beginning of *Maniac Magee,* "the history of a kid is one part fact, two parts legend, and three parts snowball. . . . [but] don't let the facts get mixed up with the truth." What is the truth of the Johnny Appleseed story? What is the truth of the Maniac Magee story?

Enrichment: Illiteracy in America

According to the National Institute for Literacy, one in five people in America over the age of sixteen can't read or write more than a few words and their names. Over 40 million people can't find a street on a map, can't take a test to get a driver's license, can't fill out a health insurance form, and can't read bedtime stories to their children.

How can this be? Some people who are illiterate have slipped through the cracks of special education classes and remedial programs, in many cases graduating from high school without learning to read and write. Some students, after struggling for years, drop out of school. Many are immigrants from countries where they had no opportunity to go to school. They arrive in America neither able to speak English nor read and write in their own language. Often people who grow up without learning how to read and write had parents who were illiterate as well.

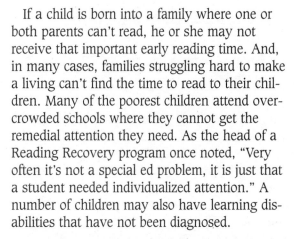

From the moment a parent holds a baby and begins reading a picture book, that child is absorbing reading lessons: what a book is, what print looks like, how it sounds, and most of all how pleasurable it is to snuggle up and enjoy a story with someone else. By the time that child is five or six, she or he will have heard hundreds and hundreds of stories and know (without actually *knowing* it) that print is read from left to right, that sentences have punctuation, and what many words look like. Before any real reading lessons begin, much of what a child needs to know to begin reading has been learned.

If a child is born into a family where one or both parents can't read, he or she may not receive that important early reading time. And, in many cases, families struggling hard to make a living can't find the time to read to their children. Many of the poorest children attend overcrowded schools where they cannot get the remedial attention they need. As the head of a Reading Recovery program once noted, "Very often it's not a special ed problem, it is just that a student needed individualized attention." A number of children may also have learning disabilities that have not been diagnosed.

Many people who are illiterate learn early how to hide the fact that they don't know how to read. At restaurants they might say, "I'll have what he's having." If they can't fill out a form, they may say they left their glasses at home and then get help filling out the form before they bring it back. In addition, they may excel at remembering all kinds of information the rest of us would write down such as directions, phone numbers, and recipes.

A number of organizations—from small church groups to Literacy Volunteers of America, which provides free tutoring to more than 70,000 people a year—are available to help people who are illiterate. While the different groups have various methods for teaching people how to read, almost all of them include individual tutors who give their students one-on-one attention.

As you read *Maniac Magee*, think about why Grayson never learned to read. How do you think he managed? Why is he finally able to learn with Maniac?

Enrichment: Segregation

"The East End was blacks, the West End was whites."

After the Civil War and the emancipation of African-Americans from slavery, many Southern states passed laws requiring the separation of whites from "persons of colour." Black people and white people could not go to the same schools, parks, theaters, or restaurants. Even cemeteries were segregated. Called "Jim Crow" laws (after a character that was used to make fun of blacks), they also forbade blacks and whites from sharing transportation, bathrooms, and later, even drinking fountains.

In 1892, an African-American man from Louisiana named Homer Plessy sat in the "whites only" section of a train (more than sixty years before Rosa Parks!) and was arrested when he refused to move. Plessy argued in court that he knew he'd disobeyed the law, but that the law went against the Constitution of the United States, particularly the Fourteenth Amendment. That amendment says no state can make a law which limits the "privileges or immunities" of a U.S. citizen. The case went through the state courts and finally reached the Supreme Court, where it was decided that it was the "natural order" of things for the races to be separated. The court said that as long as the facilities (the schools, trains, stores, and so on) were "equal," segregation did not break the law. The case of *Plessy v. Ferguson* confirmed the idea of "separate but equal" that was then used to justify segregation.

While there were no laws to enforce segregation in the North, it nevertheless existed. Neighborhoods were rarely racially mixed, nor were schools, stores, churches, restaurants, and parks. It was easier for African-Americans to vote in a few of the Northern cities, but that rarely brought about any real change. It was very difficult for African-Americans to enter politics in the North or to enter into other traditionally white leadership roles.

During the 1950s, many lawyers, both black and white, began to challenge segregation. Thurgood Marshall, an African-American lawyer who would later serve on the Supreme Court, argued in *Brown v. Board of Education of Topeka* that there was no such thing as "separate but equal" schools. Again and again, he showed how segregation made one section of the population feel inferior and that many factors made education unequal for African-Americans and so denied equal opportunities to them. Marshall won the case, and the door was opened to dismantle the rest of the segregation laws.

During the 1960s, Martin Luther King, Jr. led the non-violent civil rights movement in the South. As a result of these efforts, a Civil Rights Act was passed in 1957 and an act protecting voting rights in 1965. Still, mobs tried to prevent the integration of schools and public facilities throughout the South. Television, radio, and newspapers reported on the struggles of these civil-rights advocates. Eventually, busloads of civil-rights supporters from the Northeast arrived to help integrate the South. Still, the North and other parts of the country had their own problems with integration. In the mid-sixties, a series of race riots broke out in Los Angeles, Newark, and Detroit that destroyed whole neighborhoods.

Affirmative Action, which really began with the Civil Rights Act, was an active effort on the part of the federal government to improve employment and educational opportunities for minority groups and women. By the 1970s, however, there was already concern that favoring minorities might create "reverse discrimination."

Since the civil rights movement, few people advocate segregation. Nevertheless, it continues to exist, as does racism. Many neighborhoods and schools are still not racially mixed. *Maniac Magee* takes place in Two Mills, Pennsylvania, but when does it take place? Why does Jerry Spinelli choose to leave out that information?

Name _____ **Date** _____

Maniac Magee
Before Reading the Book

Reading Strategy: Browsing

When you browse through a book, you look at the illustrations and text on the front and back covers. You leaf through the book and read the chapter titles. As you browse through *Maniac Magee,* jot down any questions you have. For instance, why do you think the author has divided the book into parts and chapters?

Writing in Your Literature Response Journal

A. **Write about one of these topics in your journal. Circle the topic you chose.**

1. Look at the list of questions you wrote down after browsing through *Maniac Magee.* Choose one of the questions to write about.

2. Describe the most famous kid in your school or your neighborhood. You don't have to know him or her, just the stories. What is this kid supposed to have done? Why is he or she so well known? Do you think all the stories are true?

3. What does the word *home* mean to you? How is it different from *house*? Where is the place that you are most "at home?" Describe it.

4. Write about racism—either what you've noticed or actually experienced. Where do you think racism comes from? How can we stop racism?

B. **What were your predictions, questions, observations, and connections about the book? Write about one of them in your journal. Check the response you chose.**

❑ Prediction   ❑ Question   ❑ Observation   ❑ Connection

Literature Circle Guide for *Maniac Magee* • Scholastic Professional Books

Name _____   Date _____

Maniac Magee
Before Reading the Book

For Your Discussion Group

✳ Who are you? Take some time to answer the
question as honestly as you can in your
Literature Response Journal. Then make a
list of all the different groups you are part
of—including your gender, religion, ethnicity, and interests. Do people ever assume
things about you just because you are a girl, a Catholic, or Hispanic, or because you
like to read books? What assumptions do they make?

✳ Come together as a group and talk about what you wrote. Discuss the differences
between who you are and how you're treated sometimes because of certain stereo-
types. As always in your literature groups, be respectful of other people's experiences
and opinions.

✳ Now go back and look at yourself again. Do you ever assume things about other
people based on their religion or where they live or the color of their skin? Talk about
these assumptions with the group and about what you all can do to stop stereotyping
other people.

Write down any other questions your group has.

_____

_____

_____

_____

_____

_____

Literature Circle Guide for *Maniac Magee* • Scholastic Professional Books

Name _____   Date _____

Maniac Magee
Before the Story and Chapter 1

Reading Strategy: Permission to Be Confused

A lot of books are confusing when you first start to read
them. You don't know who the characters are or what's happening. This book, which
starts at ninety miles an hour, might make you feel especially confused. Don't worry if
the story doesn't make sense to you yet. Eventually it will. Good readers have faith that
any confusion will soon be cleared up. For now, hold on to your hat and enjoy the ride!

Writing in Your Literature Response Journal

A. **Write about one of these topics in your journal. Circle the topic you chose.**

1. Think about which parts of the story are confusing so far. Make a list of questions
to return to as you read. Share your questions with your literature circle, too.

2. Has something very exciting or scary or wonderful ever happened to you—
something that made you rush home and want to tell everybody everything all at
once? If so, try imagining you feel that way right now, but instead of letting the
words tumble out of your mouth, see if you can let them pour out onto paper.
Write as much as you can and as fast as you can. Like Jerry Spinelli, have fun
with the words!

3. What do you think about what Jeffrey does after "Talk to the Animals"? Have you
ever felt that way? What prompted those feelings? What did *you* want to say?

B. **What were your predictions, questions, observations, and connections as you
read? Write about one of them in your journal. Check the response you chose.**

❏ Prediction   ❏ Question   ❏ Observation   ❏ Connection

Literature Circle Guide for *Maniac Magee* • Scholastic Professional Books

Name _____ **Date** _____

Maniac Magee
Before the Story and Chapter 1

For Your Discussion Group

". . . the history of a kid is one part fact, two parts legend, and three parts snowball. And if you want to know what it was like back when Maniac Magee roamed these parts, well, just run your hand under your movie seat and be very, very careful not to let the facts get mixed up with the truth."

✳ Each group member should write down three things that he or she has done or that has happened to him or her. One of the things should be 100% true, the next should be an exaggeration but *sort of* true, and the last should be a wonderful lie—it *could* be true, it *should* be true, but it's not.

✳ Take turns sharing the three things with the rest of the group. See if anyone can guess which is which—which is true, which is exaggerated, and which is an outright lie. Then discuss what you learned about each other. What did you learn from the exaggerations and lies? Were any of the lies believable, and if so, why did you believe them? Can there be truth in lies?

✳ Finally, talk about the passage from *Maniac Magee* that appears above. What does it mean? What do you think about the passage?

Writer's Craft: The Music of Language

Someone once said that all writing aspires to music. As important as the meanings of words are, their sounds and rhythms can create emotion in a reader. Read aloud the section at the beginning of *Maniac Magee* entitled "Before the Story." Savor the vowels and the syllables as you say each word, and make sure you honor the pauses at the end of sentences and at the end of paragraphs. Can you feel the excitement and the energy, the waterfalls of words, and then the dramatic stops?

Literature Circle Guide for *Maniac Magee* • Scholastic Professional Books

Name _____ Date _____

Maniac Magee
Chapters 2–6

Reading Strategy: Making Connections

All readers put themselves into a story. For instance, a character may remind you of someone you know, or certain feelings and situations in the book may seem familiar to you. What's familiar to you in the story so far?

Writing in Your Literature Response Journal

A. Write about one of these topics in your journal. Circle the topic you chose.

1. What kinds of personal connections have you made to the book? How have you responded to the use of nicknames, Finsterwald's place, the Pickwell's dinner, or Amanda's suitcase?

2. Jerry Spinelli loves lists. Have you noticed? Look at the lists of books in Amanda's suitcase or the list of all the people at the Pickwell's dinner table. How does Jerry Spinelli make these lists so funny? Try writing some lists as if you were the author. Record in detail what's in your backpack, inside your locker, on top of your bureau or under your bed. Remember, like all writers, you can always bend the truth a little.

3. What do you notice about Maniac's running? Write everything you've noticed, even those things you think might be obvious. Do you have any questions about his running?

B. What were your predictions, questions, observations, and connections as you read? Write about one of them in your journal. Check the response you chose.

❑ Prediction   ❑ Question   ❑ Observation   ❑ Connection

Literature Circle Guide for *Maniac Magee* • Scholastic Professional Books

Name _____   Date _____

Maniac Magee
Chapters 2–6

For Your Discussion Group

❋ Some books are so much fun that we may
find ourselves reading them aloud to our
family and friends because we want to
share the laughter. What's your favorite
scene so far? Share it with the group.

❋ Each person should share a favorite scene or passage. It's all right if two or more
people share the same one.

❋ After discussing everyone's choices, talk about what you like most about the book so
far. You may find you want to focus on the passages that you read aloud. How does
the writing contribute to your enjoyment of these passages?

Writer's Craft: Word Derivations

*"fin-ster-wal-lies (fin′ster′wal-ez) n. [Two Mills, Pa., W. End] Violent trembling of the
body, especially in the extremities (arms and legs)"*

Where do new words come from? As Jerry Spinelli's made-up dictionary definition for
"finsterwallies" shows, they are often **derived** from particular places and events. In
eighteenth-century England, the Earl of Sandwich didn't want to stop gambling long
enough to eat and so, to save time, he would just put some meat between two pieces of
bread and call it a meal. Today, of course, we call that a "sandwich."

A good dictionary will always show you how to pronounce a word, what part of speech
it is, and where it comes from (its **derivation**). Look through a dictionary and find out
where some of your favorite words come from.

Literature Circle Guide for Maniac Magee • Scholastic Professional Books

Name _____ **Date** _____

Maniac Magee
Chapters 7–13

Reading Strategy: Visualizing

Jerry Spinelli loves details. He likes to show you every little moment in a scene. Such writers make it easy to imagine what they are describing: the baseball players coming up to bat as if they were "walking a gangplank," the pitcher, McNab, "breathing like a picadored bull." If you don't find yourself seeing what Spinelli is writing, read more slowly and stop occasionally to shut your eyes until you can bring the picture into focus. See it in your imagination!

Writing in Your Literature Response Journal

A. **Write about one of these topics in your journal. Circle the topic you chose.**

1. Visualize the baseball diamond, all the kids, and Magee with Amanda's book in his hand. What color is the book? Write your own description of the scene.

2. It seems like every kid in this story has a nickname or "tag." Which "tags" are your favorites? What are some of your friends' nicknames? Do you have one? If so, how did you get it?

3. Have you ever been the new kid in town? Has a new kid ever come to your school? How are new kids usually treated? What's typical about the way everyone reacts to Maniac Magee? What's special or unique about the way he reacts and is treated?

B. **What were your predictions, questions, observations, and connections as you read? Write about one of them in your journal. Check the response you chose.**

❑ Prediction ❑ Question ❑ Observation ❑ Connection

Literature Circle Guide for *Maniac Magee* • Scholastic Professional Books

Name _____ Date _____

Maniac Magee
Chapters 7–13

For Your Discussion Group

✱ Jerry Spinelli tells us a lot about what Maniac does but doesn't really indicate what he thinks about Maniac or what kind of person his main character is. He lets the readers decide that for themselves based on Maniac's actions.

✱ Have each person divide a piece of paper down the middle into two vertical columns. On one side, write "Character's Actions" and on the other write "Interpretation." Under the "Character's Actions" side, write down one thing you see Maniac doing in the story. For instance, you might write that he begs and bugs Amanda for a book. Go to the "Interpretation" side. What do you think this fact means about Maniac? What does it tell you about him? One person might say that it means he's really smart and cares about continuing to learn, even if he isn't in school. Someone else might say that Maniac really needs a friend and doesn't want Amanda to disappear. Write down what you think. Each person in the group should record at least five facts and interpretations about Maniac.

✱ Using your facts and interpretations, talk as a group about what kind of person you think Maniac Magee is. Is he stupid or smart? Does he care about others, or is he inconsiderate? What are some of his characteristics?

Writer's Craft: Verbs

"He windmilled, reared, lunged, fired . . ."

Verbs are like hearts—they pump energy into the rest of the sentence. Without them, of course, there is no sentence. When verbs are dull, no matter how exciting the rest of the words, the sentence seems flat. Jerry Spinelli uses great verbs—*windmilled, reared, lunged, fired*. What other verbs can you find in the book that surprise and dazzle you?

Literature Circle Guide for *Maniac Magee* • Scholastic Professional Books

Name _____ Date _____

Maniac Magee
Chapters 14–21

Reading Strategy: Listening to Tone

You can probably always tell when your mother is
mad at you. She can say, "Oh, I can't believe you did
that," in a tone that tells you she's frustrated, but that it does-
n't really matter. But if she were to say those words with a different tone in her voice,
you would know you were in big, big trouble. You can feel an author's tone from the
choice of words, the rhythms of the sentences, and the subject matter.

Writing in Your Literature Response Journal

A. Write about one of these topics in your journal. Circle the topic you chose.

1. Jerry Spinelli often sounds very funny and light-hearted in *Maniac Magee*, but
have you noticed different tones in his writing? Do other feelings ever poke
through the laughter? In which part of the book did you notice this?

2. Repetition—repeating a word or phrase over and over—can make writing more ener-
getic and powerful. Look at how Jerry Spinelli uses repetition in Chapters 15 and 16.
Write a paragraph or two using that kind of repetitive phrase. You might use "I love
. . ." or "I know . . ." or "I wish . . ." or another phrase of your very own.

3. *Bullies!* In both the East End and the West End, there are bullies. What do you
think makes someone a bully? Have you ever had to deal with one? Describe
what happened. Have you ever felt like being a bully yourself? Tell why.

B. What were your predictions, questions, observations, and connections as you
read? Write about one of them in your journal. Check the response you chose.

❑ Prediction   ❑ Question   ❑ Observation   ❑ Connection

Literature Circle Guide for *Maniac Magee* • Scholastic Professional Books

Name _____ **Date** _____

Maniac Magee
Chapters 14–21

For Your Discussion Group

✳ Sometimes an author includes a detail that points to a deeper meaning in the story. In *Beauty and the Beast*, for instance, the beast has a rose in his castle. That rose is symbolic of his heart. When the rose dies, he will die, too. Therefore, the rose is not just a rose.

✳ Consider with your group the following three details and think about what else they might be telling you about Maniac Magee. What are they symbolic of?

1. Maniac's skill at untying knots
2. how Maniac walks down the middle of the street after he unties the knot
3. Maniac's running

✳ Why does Maniac leave the Beales? Talk together about the different reasons.

Writer's Craft: Hyperbole

Hyperbole is a word that means intentional exaggeration. Lots of writers use hyperbole for effect. In fact, if you've ever been telling a story and decide to make the time you spent stuck on the airplane a little longer and a little scarier, you've used hyperbole, too. By now, you've probably noticed that Jerry Spinelli *loves* hyperbole. What are some examples of hyperbole that you've seen in the book?

Literature Circle Guide for *Maniac Magee* • Scholastic Professional Books

Name _____ **Date** _____

Maniac Magee
Chapters 22–26

Reading Strategy: Asking Questions

Jeffrey Magee learns a lot by asking questions. It
is especially important to ask questions, all kinds
of questions—big ones, stupid ones, obvious ones,
profound ones—when you read. The more questions
you ask about the story as you read, the more carefully you
will read and the more involved you will become. Write down your questions in your
notebook, and talk about them later in your literature circle.

Writing in Your Literature Response Journal

A. **Write about one of these topics in your journal. Circle the topic you chose.**

1. Maniac Magee asks Grayson lots and lots of questions. What questions would you
like to ask Maniac? How do you think he might respond? What do you want to
know about him? Write a list of questions in your journal.

2. Have you ever had a friendship with an older person? What do you notice about
Maniac Magee's relationship with Grayson? What does it remind you of? How
would you compare it to your friendship with someone older?

B. **What were your predictions, questions, observations, and connections as you
read? Write about one of them in your journal. Check the response you chose.**

❏ Prediction ❏ Question ❏ Observation ❏ Connection

Literature Circle Guide for *Maniac Magee* • Scholastic Professional Books

Name _____ Date _____

Maniac Magee
Chapters 22–26

For Your Discussion Group

✻ One of the best things about reading a
book with a group is that some people
may know about things others do not.
Find out if everyone in your group
understands all the baseball talk—the
pitchers, the majors, the minors, the
scouts, the rules of the game. If some-
one doesn't know much about baseball, clue him or her in. Make sure you do it in a
way that is respectful of the fact that there are some things that people don't know.
For instance, you may know about baseball, but not about soccer.

✻ Talk together about the scene where Grayson questions Magee about black people.
Is this scene realistic? Tell why or why not. Why do you think Jerry Spinelli included
this scene in the book? Does it tell you anything about the larger world in which
Jeffrey lives?

Writer's Craft: Dialogue

Whereas the first part of *Maniac Magee* is filled with freewheeling descriptions of Maniac's
exploits, the second is largely made up of the quiet and very natural conversations
between the boy and his new friend Grayson. In order to make those conversations feel
real, Spinelli writes the words in the way the characters would actually talk—*"But call me
Grayson, like ever'body."* There are many short, simple sentences that capture the gen-
uine kind of back and forth banter between two people. Note, too, that Spinelli does not
find it necessary to indicate who is speaking all the time—to always say "he said." He
trusts the reader to follow the dialogue and always know who's talking.

Literature Circle Guide for *Maniac Magee* • Scholastic Professional Books

Name _____   Date _____

Maniac Magee
Chapters 27–32

Reading Strategy: Noticing the Author's Style

As you read, one thing you may find yourself noticing without even realizing it is the author's style—the particular way she or he puts words together. You may observe that the writer uses lots of comparisons, or none at all, tells the story mostly with dialogue, or never tells you what the characters said. Sometimes an author will even change her or his style from book to book, or within a book.

Writing in Your Literature Response Journal

A. Write about one of these topics in your journal. Circle the topic you chose.

1. Compare Jerry Spinelli's styles in Part I and Part II. How are the styles similar? How do they differ? Use sample passages from the book to support your judgment.

2. Do you remember how you learned to read? Why do you think Grayson never learned? Why is Jeffrey able to teach Grayson to read?

3. On Thanksgiving Day, Jeffrey says grace. What is he thankful for? Does anything surprise you about what he says? Explain what it is and why it surprised you. What are you grateful for?

B. What were your predictions, questions, observations, and connections as you read? Write about one of them in your journal. Check the response you chose.

❑ Prediction   ❑ Question   ❑ Observation   ❑ Connection

Literature Circle Guide for *Maniac Magee* • Scholastic Professional Books

Name _____ **Date** _____

Maniac Magee
Chapters 27–32

For Your Discussion Group

✳ Talk about holidays and the way Magee and Grayson celebrate Thanksgiving and Christmas. What is typical about their festivities? What is unusual? How do their celebrations compare to the way most people celebrate the holidays? Make a list of everything Maniac and Grayson have given each other since they met.

✳ Were you prepared for the end of Part II? How did it make you feel, and why? What upsets Maniac so much at the funeral?

Writer's Craft: Comparisons

When Grayson is learning to read, Spinelli compares his troubles with the letter *c* to trying to ride a bucking bronco. Sometimes elaborate comparisons can make the story confusing—you can forget for a minute whether you are reading about an old man learning to read or a cowboy at a rodeo. That's part of the fun of comparisons in writing; they let you have both images in your mind at once. They make you feel just how hard and wild learning to read is and how tough and persistent Grayson is—more so than if all you saw in your imagination was a man sitting at a table with a book. What other comparisons do you notice Jerry Spinelli using?

Literature Circle Guide for *Maniac Magee* • Scholastic Professional Books

Name _____ Date _____

Maniac Magee
Chapters 33–38

Reading Strategy: Making Predictions

As a character, Maniac Magee is pretty unpredictable; it's hard to imagine what he might do next. By now, you may be wondering what is going to happen at the end of the story. Where do you think it's going? What makes you think so? When you ask yourself those questions, you often begin to pay closer attention to what's happening right now in the book. You try to find clues that will help you figure out what is going to happen next.

Writing in Your Literature Response Journal

A. **Write about one of these topics in your journal. Circle the topic you chose.**

1. What do you think will happen to Maniac's relationships with the McNabs, Mars Bar, and/or the Beales? Explain what kinds of questions, clues, and personal experience you used to make your predictions.

2. Look at the first sentence of Chapter 34. How does it make you feel? What if Spinelli had described a warm, spring day? Would it have made you feel the same way? Write about a time when you were sad or angry or happy, but do not describe how you felt. Instead, describe the weather and make it express your mood.

2. What is Maniac Magee's most powerful memory? Why is it so powerful? Is it something he saw or just imagined? What is your most powerful memory? Write about it.

B. **What were your predictions, questions, observations, and connections as you read? Write about one of them in your journal. Check the response you chose.**

❏ Prediction   ❏ Question   ❏ Observation   ❏ Connection

Literature Circle Guide for *Maniac Magee* • Scholastic Professional Books

Name _____   Date _____

Maniac Magee
Chapters 33–38

For Your Discussion Group

"No one else would orphan him."

❋ The quote above appears on the last
   page of chapter 33 (page 123).
   Reread the chapter, and then discuss
   the following questions: What does
   Maniac mean when he thinks that?
   How many times has he been
   orphaned? What do you think could
   heal that terrible feeling inside him?

❋ Again and again, Maniac does things that all the other kids are scared to do. Go back
   to the beginning of the book. Make a list of all the things he should be scared of but
   isn't. Examine your list. What does this tell you about Maniac? Why isn't he scared of
   these things? Is there any thing that he *is* scared of? What is it?

Writer's Craft: Semi-colons

"They weren't raisins; they were roaches."

If two sentences express ideas that are closely related, you can use a semicolon to separate them. As you read, notice how often Jerry Spinelli uses semicolons. Write two separate and complete sentences for the sentence above. Say the original sentence several
times. Pay attention to the flow of the sentence. Then repeat the two new sentences several times. How does the flow of the two sentences compare to the original sentence?

Literature Circle Guide for *Maniac Magee* • Scholastic Professional Books

Name _____ Date _____

Maniac Magee
Chapters 39–46

Reading Strategy: Summarizing

So much happens in *Maniac Magee*. The book is crammed with
detail and activity. To keep the story straight in your head, at
the end of each chapter ask yourself, "What is the most important thing that happened
in this chapter?" For instance, after Chapter 43, you might note to yourself, "Maniac is
sleeping at different houses all over town." Many other things are happening in this little
poetic chapter, but summarizing can help you keep track of the main events of the story.

Writing in Your Literature Response Journal

A. Write about one of these topics in your journal. Circle the topic you chose.

1. Summarize one of the chapters in this section. Reread the chapter, and then jot
down what happened. Remember to list the events in the order in which they
occurred in the story.

2. Copy into your journal one of your favorite paragraphs or passages from the book.
As you write, become aware of the length of the sentences and the feel of the
words. Why did you choose this passage? What do you like about it? What do
you like about the writing?

3. What is the biggest problem in your life? Do you think Maniac could solve it?
How would he solve it? Write a scene where you imagine Maniac in your home
and in your town.

**B. What were your predictions, questions, observations, and connections as you
read? Write about one of them in your journal. Check the response you chose.**

❏ Prediction   ❏ Question   ❏ Observation   ❏ Connection

Literature Circle Guide for *Maniac Magee* • Scholastic Professional Books

Name _____ **Date** _____

Maniac Magee
Chapters 39–46

For Your Discussion Group

✻ Talk about the relationship between Mars Bar and Maniac. Why does Mars initially not like Maniac? How do they manage to become friends?

✻ Individually, make a list of all the "knots" that Maniac unties during the course of the story. What are all the problems that he solves both for other people and for himself, from the beginning of the story to the end? Then share and combine your lists. Which knot do you think was hardest for Maniac to untie, and why?

Writer's Craft: Clichés

A sly fox, a busy bee, a silly goose. We are so used to hearing these words together that we could almost fill in the blanks if one of them were missing. Phrases that are this predictable and tired are called **clichés**. Compare them to the way Jerry Spinelli combines words:

"One morning in early July, cruising down the appleskin hour, Maniac thought he heard footsteps other than his own."

"The appleskin hour." You can almost see the soft pinks and whites curved around the horizon. Have you ever heard the sky described that way before? The challenge for a writer is to say things in ways that seem both perfect and fresh. Do you think Jerry Spinelli accomplishes that? Is his language ever clichéd?

Literature Circle Guide for *Maniac Magee* • Scholastic Professional Books

Maniac Magee
After Reading

When parents pick a name for their baby, they have many things to consider. What famous people have had that name? For instance, since the rise and fall of Nazi Germany, few people call their children Adolph anymore. The meaning of the name is important, too—does it mean wisdom or heartache? Parents must think of all the associations or **allusions** connected to the name they choose.

A writer also thinks about what to name characters, and sometimes places. He or she may make deliberate references to other stories, famous characters, or historical events. For instance, when Jerry Spinelli calls the bully Mars Bar, it's both funny to imagine him with a candy bar sticking out of his mouth, and frightening to envision him as Mars, the Roman God of War.

In *Maniac Magee*, Jerry Spinelli makes a number of allusions to other stories. Reading these stories will tell you more about what he intended with this story. You'll know more about what happens in the book and why. The allusions may be as direct as the name of a book or a famous place, but sometimes you may have to do some research to realize what Jerry Spinelli is referring to.

Research the following topics to shed more light on *Maniac Magee*. Write about them in your literature response journals, and then discuss them in your literature circle.

✳ Maniac borrows a book from Amanda about the Children's Crusade. What is the Children's Crusade? What does it have in common with *Maniac Magee*?

✳ Why does Jerry Spinelli have Maniac read *Lyle, Lyle Crocodile* to the Beale children the first night? What is that book about? What does it tell you about Maniac?

✳ In Part III, Maniac ends up in Valley Forge. What happened at Valley Forge? Why does Spinelli choose to put Maniac there at that point in the story?

✳ Research the Gordian Knot. How does it change your understanding of the end of Part 1?

✳ Read about the Roman god Mars. Why does Jerry Spinelli use Mars Bars to allude to this Roman god?

Literature Circle Guide for *Maniac Magee* • Scholastic Professional Books

Individual Projects

1. Read about some legendary American heroes—Pecos Bill, Bess Call, John Henry, Paul Bunyan. Then create your own folk hero—maybe even based upon someone you know in your school or your community. Let yourself exaggerate and have fun.

2. Write to Jerry Spinelli. What did you want to say to him while you were reading the book? Do you find that you still have questions or strong opinions you want to share with him? The more specific you are about what you have to say, and the more genuinely curious your questions, the more likely he will write you back. Write to Jerry Spinelli in care of his publisher. You can find the address at the front of the book.

3. Listen to the story of an older person—a neighbor, a grandparent, or a family friend. What has happened in this person's life? Look at the kinds of questions Maniac Magee asks Grayson. Make sure to listen carefully. Know when to encourage the person to continue talking. Make your older friend a book filled with his or her stories.

Group Projects

1. Work out a plan with a kindergarten or first-grade teacher to pair your group with children in lower grades as reading buddies. Share your favorite picture books with your group. Read them aloud to each other before you visit your younger buddies.

2. *Maniac Magee* would make a super play. Select your favorite group scene—the untying of the knot, the hitting of all the baseballs, the race with Mars Bar—that allows everyone in the group to play a part. Read over the scene together and decide what lines you will keep. Will you need to add any text to explain the action? Think about the action and how you will show it. After everyone in your group has a part, memorize your lines, practice, and then share it with the whole class.

3. Learn about the history of segregation and civil rights in your community. Go to the library and read old newspapers. If your community has a history center, visit it and talk to the people there. Interview older people. Then think about your community today. Have things changed? How did these changes occur? What else still needs to happen? Create a bulletin board for the class when you have completed your research.

Literature Circle Guide for *Maniac Magee* • Scholastic Professional Books